MOONBEAR'S SUNRISE

A MOONBEAR Book

• FRANK ASCH •

ALADDIN

NEW YORK   LONDON   TORONTO   SYDNEY   NEW DELHI

ALADDIN

An imprint of Simon & Schuster Children's Publishing Division

1230 Avenue of the Americas, New York, NY 10020

First Aladdin hardcover edition March 2014

For information about special discounts for bulk purchases, please contact

Simon & Schuster Special Sales at 1-866-506-1949 or business@simonandschuster.com.

The Simon & Schuster Speakers Bureau can bring authors to your live event.

For more information or to book an event contact the Simon & Schuster Speakers Bureau

at 1-866-248-3049 or visit our website at www.simonspeakers.com.

The text of this book was set in Olympian LT Std.

The illustrations for this book were rendered digitally.

Manufactured in China 1213 SCP

10 9 8 7 6 5 4 3 2 1

Library of Congress Cataloging-in-Publication Data

Asch, Frank, author, illustrator.

Moonbear's sunrise / Frank Asch. — First Aladdin hardcover edition.

pages cm. — (Moonbear)

Summary: When Bear tries to see the sunrise but always oversleeps, Little Bird makes a suggestion.

ISBN 978-1-4424-6647-0 (hc)

[1. Sun—Rising and setting—Fiction. 2. Bedtime—Fiction. 3. Bears—Fiction. 4. Birds—Fiction.] I. Title.

PZ7.A778Mos 2014

[E]—dc23

2013024840

ISBN 978-1-4424-6658-6 (eBook)

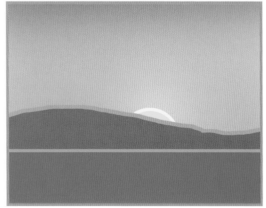
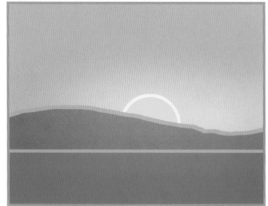

To Pacifique

 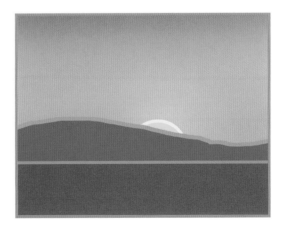

One evening Bear and Little Bird were watching the moon come up over the mountains.

"Isn't moonrise beautiful!" cried Bear, and he felt so happy he jumped up and danced a little dance.

"Moonrise reminds me of sunrise," said Little Bird. "That's beautiful too!"

"Gosh, I don't think I've ever seen the sun come up," replied Bear.

"That's because you stay up so late at night watching the moon," chirped Little Bird. "When the sun comes up, you're always fast asleep."

The next day Bear walked downtown and bought himself an alarm clock.

That night, after moon watching for many hours, he wound up the clock and set it to go off early in the morning. *Now I'll be able to wake up and see the sunrise*, thought Bear as he fell asleep.

But when the alarm went off, Bear was so sleepy he kept right on snoozing.

That afternoon Bear bought himself *another* alarm clock.

After staying up late watching the moon again, he set *both* alarm clocks. *Now I'll wake up for sure!* he thought.

The next morning the alarm clocks rang loudly, but Bear kept right on snoozing.

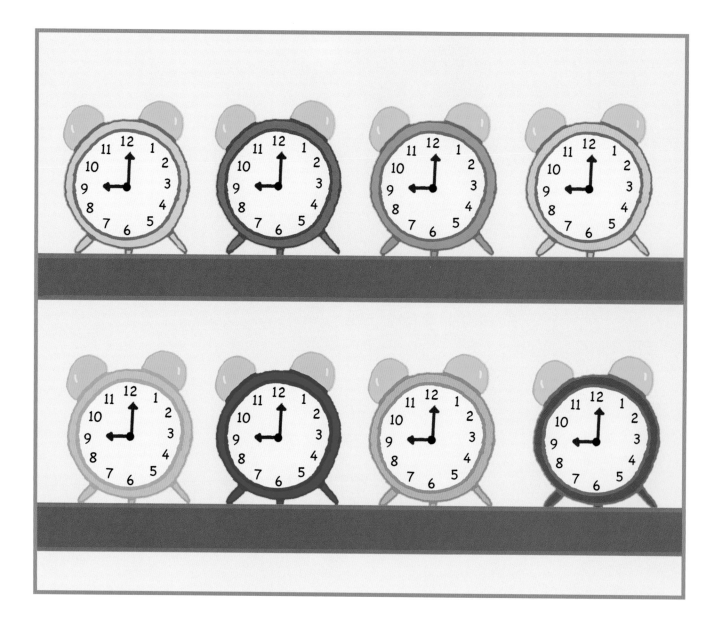

I guess two alarm clocks weren't loud enough, thought Bear.

So back to the store he went, and he bought himself eight more alarm clocks!

When all ten alarm clocks went off at the same time the next morning, they made a very loud racket.

But . . . Bear kept right on snoozing.

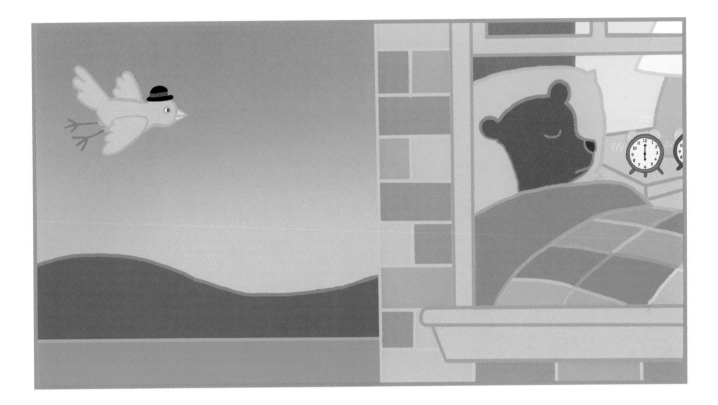

That afternoon Bear went to visit Little Bird. "Little Bird, will you wake me up tomorrow morning so I can see the sunrise?"

"Sure," chirped Little Bird. "I'd be glad to."

Once again Bear stayed up very late watching the moon.

Early in the morning Little Bird woke up and flew over to Bear's house.

"Wake up! Wake up, Bear!" chirped Little Bird.
But Bear kept right on snoozing.

So Little Bird flew outside, found an acorn, and . . .

dropped it on Bear's head!

But Bear kept right on snoozing.

I know! thought Little Bird, and he pecked Bear on the nose.

"Wake up, you sleepyhead!" chirped Little Bird.

But Bear would not wake up!

Later that morning when Bear finally got out of bed, the sun was already high in the sky.

"Why didn't you wake me like you promised?" he asked Little Bird. "Don't you care if I ever see the sunrise?"

"I *tried*! I even pecked your nose," chirped Little Bird, "but you were too sleepy!"

That night Bear invited Little Bird over for some moon watching.

They hadn't watched the moon for very long when Little Bird said, "Time for bed!"

"Don't be silly!" exclaimed Bear. "We've only just begun to watch the moon."

"That's true," said Little Bird. "But if you want to wake up early, you have to go to bed early."

"But I'm not tired," complained Bear.

"Never mind that!" said Little Bird, and he marched Bear
to his bed.

"Now get under the covers!" insisted Little Bird.

As soon as Bear put his head on the pillow, he fell fast asleep.

The next morning Bear woke up very early.

He jumped out of bed and ran outside.

Just then, the sun was rising over the mountains.